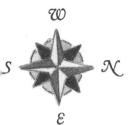

W
S — N
E

BALTIC SEA
RUSSIA LITHUANIA
KALININGRAD
GERMANY
POLAND
VISTULA RIVER
BELARUS
CZECH REPUBLIC
SLOVAKIA UKRAINE

BAY OF
GDAŃSK

GDAŃSK •

• TCZEW

BALTIC SEA

Rescued by R/V *Baltica* on
Monday, January 25, 2010

Little Dog Lost

The True Story of a Brave Dog Named Baltic

Mônica Carnesi

Nancy Paulsen Books ◉ An Imprint of Penguin Group (USA) Inc.

This book is dedicated to the members of the crew of the R/V *Baltica*
in recognition of their bravery and compassion.

NANCY PAULSEN BOOKS · A division of Penguin Young Readers Group.
Published by The Penguin Group. Penguin Group (USA) Inc., 375 Hudson Street, New York, NY 10014, U.S.A.
Penguin Group (Canada), 90 Eglinton Avenue East, Suite 700, Toronto, Ontario M4P 2Y3, Canada (a division of Pearson Penguin Canada Inc.).
Penguin Books Ltd, 80 Strand, London WC2R 0RL, England.
Penguin Ireland, 25 St. Stephen's Green, Dublin 2, Ireland (a division of Penguin Books Ltd.).
Penguin Group (Australia), 250 Camberwell Road, Camberwell, Victoria 3124, Australia (a division of Pearson Australia Group Pty Ltd).
Penguin Books India Pvt Ltd, 11 Community Centre, Panchsheel Park, New Delhi - 110 017, India.
Penguin Group (NZ), 67 Apollo Drive, Rosedale, Auckland 0632, New Zealand (a division of Pearson New Zealand Ltd).
Penguin Books (South Africa) (Pty) Ltd, 24 Sturdee Avenue, Rosebank, Johannesburg 2196, South Africa.
Penguin Books Ltd, Registered Offices: 80 Strand, London WC2R 0RL, England.

Design by Marikka Tamura. Text set P22 Mayflower . The art was done in watercolor, pen and ink on Fabriano hot-pressed paper.
Library of Congress Cataloging-in-Publication Data is available upon request.
ISBN 978-0-399-25666-0
1 3 5 7 9 10 8 6 4 2

On a very cold day, during a very cold winter, sheets of ice float on the Vistula River and out toward the Baltic Sea.

Something is moving in the water!
What is it?

Is it a bird?
No.
A fish?
No.

It's a DOG!

A little dog is adrift on the ice!

"Can anybody help? Please, help Dog!"

The firemen come to help.

They go into the river,
trying to
reach Dog.

But the river flows too fast. The little dog floats away with the current,

past the people and past the buildings. Dog leaves everyone behind.

Night comes and goes.

Dog's thick fur keeps him warm.
But Dog is wet and tired and hungry.
And he is scared.

Don't be scared, Dog!

A ship is coming!

The crew sees something on the ice.

Is it a seal?

No.

It has four legs, ears, and a tail.

"It's a dog! Let's help him!"

The crew pulls out a big net on a pole.
Jump in, Dog!

But Dog slips.
He falls into the water.

Oh no! Where is Dog?

There he is!
Dog climbs back onto the ice.

The crew lowers a small boat into the icy water.
A seaman climbs in and paddles toward Dog.

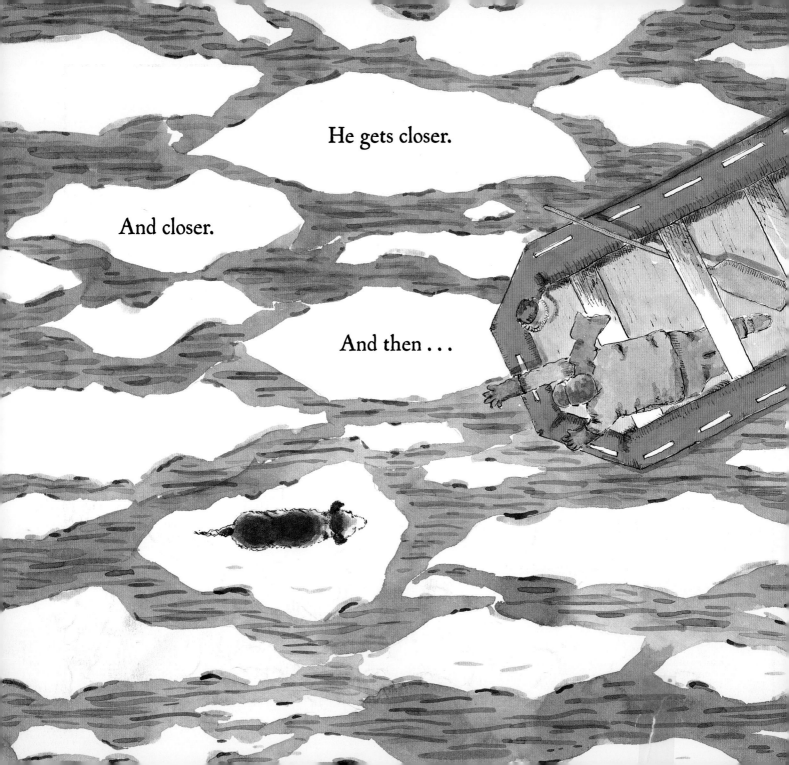

He saves Dog!

"Quick, get towels!
Quick, get blankets!"
The whole crew helps Dog.

Is Dog okay?

Dog is so weak and so tired, he can barely move.

Finally, Dog is warm.
Finally, Dog is dry.

He eats and falls asleep, safe at last aboard the ship.

When Dog wakes up,
he looks for the people who saved him.

They are eating
breakfast.
Everyone is happy
to see Dog awake.
They give Dog
a sausage.

Dog finds the man who pulled him out of the water.
Dog puts his nose on his lap.

That's how he says "Thank you."

"You're welcome, Dog.
You're welcome . . . Baltic!
That's it! That's what we'll call you!"

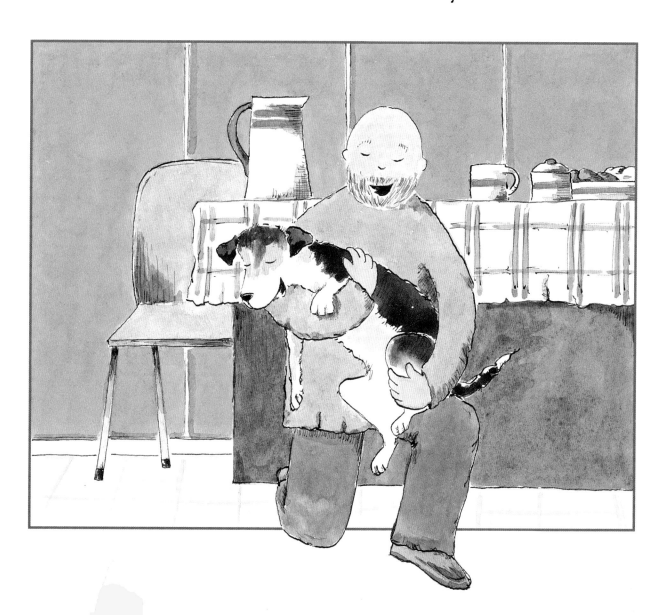

And that's how a brave little dog got his name and his new home.

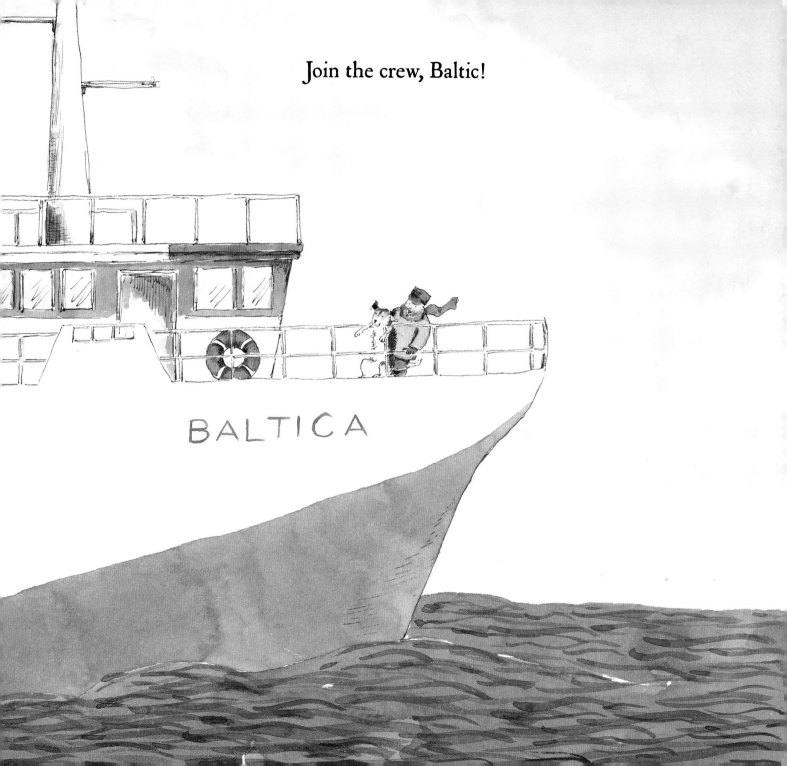

Join the crew, Baltic!

A NOTE FROM THE AUTHOR

On Saturday, January 23, 2010, a dog was seen floating on an ice floe on the Vistula River near the city of Grudziadz, Poland, 60 miles inland from the Bay of Gdańsk in the Baltic Sea. No one knows exactly where or how the dog first got trapped on the ice.

According to news reports, firefighters from Grudziadz attempted to save him, without success. Against all odds, the dog was able to remain afloat on the ice for two days, and with his thick fur coat he was able to survive one of Poland's coldest winter spells. On Monday, January 25, 2010, the dog was spotted by the crew of R/V *Baltica*, a scientific research vessel, 15 miles from land on the Baltic Sea.

Attempts to rescue the dog began immediately but proved difficult. Moving the ship close to the floe caused the ice to shift, and as a result, the dog fell into the water several times. Anxious to reach the dog before it drowned, the crew lowered a small pontoon boat driven by the ship's watch engineer officer, Adam Buczynski. Using a grappling iron, he was able to get close enough to the ice floe to pull the dog to safety.

Nicknamed "Baltic," the dog quickly became attached to members of the crew. Once all attempts to find his original owners failed, Baltic was adopted by Officer Buczynski (pictured). He is now an official member of the R/V *Baltica* crew and has participated in a number of research missions. When at sea, he enjoys sitting on the bridge, watching the water and seagulls.

The story of Baltic's adventure and rescue made news all over the world.

First spotted
on Saturday,
January 23, 2010

NOWE

GRUDZIADZ

GNIEW

VISTULA (Wisla) RIVER

Baltic's travels
on the Vistula River